Chat Room

Kristin Butcher

Orca currents

ORCA BOOK PUBLISHERS

Library and Archives Canada Cataloguing in Publication

Butcher, Kristin

Chat room / Kristin Butcher.

(Orca currents)

ISBN 1-55143-529-2 (bound) ISBN 1-55143-485-7 (pbk.)

I. Title. II. Series.

PS8553.U6972C43 2006   jC813'.54   C2006-900469-2

Summary: Is Linda the victim of mistaken identity?

First published in the United States, 2006
Library of Congress Control Number: 2006921144

Orca Book Publishers gratefully acknowledges the support for its publishing
programs provided by the following agencies: the Government of Canada
through the Book Publishing Industry Development Program (BPIDP), the
Canada Council for the Arts, and the British Columbia Arts Council.

Cover design: Lynn O'Rourke
Cover photography: Getty Images

Orca Book Publishers
PO Box 5626, Stn. B
Victoria, BC Canada
V8R 6S4

Orca Book Publishers
PO Box 468
Custer, WA USA
98240-0468

www.orcabook.com
Printed and bound in Canada
Printed on 50% post-consumer recycled paper,
processed chlorine free using vegetable, low VOC inks.

09 08 07 06 5 4 3 2 1

For Donna,
who understands the most important
part of chatting is listening.

chapter one

Back in elementary school, assemblies meant sitting on the floor. In high school things are different. Because we're older now, we sit in actual chairs—at least that's the theory. If you're one of the first people into the gym, the system works fine. But I always arrive after every seat's been taken. If there's not a person sitting in it, it's being saved for someone. Basically, it's a school-wide version of musical chairs, and I've always sucked at that game.

Take Friday's assembly. The gym was packed as usual, but for once it looked like I was going to get lucky. There was an empty seat at the end of the third row. I would have preferred something a little farther back, but it was that or nothing. So I grabbed it.

Unfortunately Janice saw me and started waving from the middle of the row. I wanted to pretend I didn't see her, but I knew if I did she'd unleash that bullhorn voice of hers, and in two seconds I'd have every kid in school staring at me. So I bumped my way through the line of knees separating us and shriveled into the seat beside her.

"What class are you missing?" Whispering wasn't a skill Janice had ever learned, and, even though everyone around us was talking, her voice drowned them out.

"Math," I said, shrinking a little deeper into my chair. I intentionally avoided asking her what she was missing, but that didn't stop Janice.

"It's biology for me. *Thank God*! If I had to miss band I'd be ticked, but I can definitely do without forty minutes of Bio-Bernstein droning on about reproduction. What have they dragged us in here for anyway?"

I shrugged. "I don't know. The gym riot maybe? There are posters about it up all over school." I nodded toward a group of students huddled around the microphone. "It looks like student council's running the assembly, so I bet that's what it is."

Janice rolled her eyes and flopped back in her chair. "Oh, joy! Just what we need —another chance for Wellington High's favored few to show off."

I wasn't sure if Janice was referring to the gym riot or student council running the assembly. Probably both. She was against everything social.

Janice Beastly was queen of the grumps. Her real name was *Beasley*, but she was so negative and in-your-face that everybody called her Beastly. It didn't

3

help that she was built like a wrestler with a voice to match. She didn't have a lot of friends. None, actually, unless you counted me.

Even that was only friendship by default. I didn't like Janice any more than anyone else did, but when she showed up at the start of grade nine, she adopted me. And since her locker was right beside mine, I was stuck.

Maybe I should have been grateful, because except for Janice, I don't have many friends either. Not that people hate me. At least I don't think they do. I'm just not part of any crowd.

The microphone squealed.

"Sorry about that," said the boy standing in front of it. It was Marc Solomon, student council president and one of the most popular guys in school. He grinned. "But now that I have your attention, let's get this party started. The first thing on today's agenda is the big gym riot coming up next Friday."

Behind him the student council started

clapping and cheering, and in a matter of seconds the audience joined in.

Marc leaned into the mic. "That's the spirit, Wellington!"

"Oh, spare me," Janice muttered.

Marc held up his hands for quiet. "As always, the riot's going to be a blast, and this year we've added a whole bunch of new events like tricycle basketball, egg toss and a chain-gang relay."

"What's that?" someone hollered.

Marc grinned again. "I'll get to that. That and all the other details." He turned and gestured toward a pretty blond girl standing behind him. She smiled and waved. "Thanks to our student council vice-president, the teachers have agreed to give us gym riot planning time," he paused, "last period this afternoon."

"Hey, that's my band class!" Janice protested, but her complaint was lost in the roar that erupted around us.

When it got quiet again, Marc motioned for a boy in the front row to join him at the microphone. Hesitantly, the kid stood up. It was Chad Sharp. I recognized him from French class.

"Right now, though, I want to tell you about a totally new and exciting feature that's just been added to the school's website." Marc clapped Chad on the back. "And this guy here is the mastermind behind it. For those of you who don't know him, let me introduce Chad Sharp."

There was a bit of applause, and Chad's cheeks went red. I felt sorry for him. If I had to stand up in front of a thousand kids, I'd probably die.

Marc gestured for Chad to take over the mic, but Chad shook his head.

"A man of big ideas, but few words," Marc said, resuming his spot in front of the microphone. "But that's okay. The important thing is that thanks to Chad and the parent council, we now have a chat room on our school website."

An instant buzz spread through the gym.

"You heard right." Marc nodded.

"A chat room. Actually, it's lots of chat rooms. There's something for everybody. If you want to compare notes about movies or music or the newest fads, you can visit *The Hot Spot*. For you athletic types, there's a sports chat room. Want to talk about the stuff going on at school? Go to the *Wellington Room*. If you just need to let off steam, there's a chat room for that too. There's even a *Homework Help* chat room."

Excited pockets of chatter sprang up around the gym, and it took Marc a good minute to get everyone quiet again.

"There will be some rules, of course," he said. "This could be a really good thing, so we don't want anybody messing it up."

"What kind of rules?" someone asked.

"Well, for starters, only Wellington students will have access. Secondly, when you enter a chat room you have to use a nickname. And thirdly, you can't gross out or talk about other students."

A hand went up. "If your identity is secret, how will anyone know if you're breaking the rules?"

"Good question," Marc said. "The office will monitor the chat rooms. When you log on, you'll exchange your student number and e-mail address for a nickname. No one will have access to your personal information except the site administrator—a.k.a. Mr. Barnes in computer science. To everyone online, you'll be anonymous. But if you break the rules, the office will track you down and you'll be toast. Any other questions?"

Hands shot up all over the place.

"This is the stupidest thing I've ever heard," Janice grumbled, making it impossible for me to hear the questions and answers. Even a glare from the girl in front of Janice didn't shut her up. "I can't believe the principal is going along with this lame idea. Chat rooms are nothing but hangouts for perverts. Anybody who visits them is asking for trouble."

chapter two

"You're going to do it, aren't you?"

I shrugged, feeling defensive. Janice was getting to me. "I haven't decided yet."

"Yes, you have. You just don't want to admit it." She shook her head in disgust. She probably would have stalked off if she could have. We were penned in by kids exiting the gym so she simply looked away.

"Why are you so against it?"

That was the wrong thing to say. Janice was in my face before I even finished the sentence.

"Have you heard anything I've said?"

"You don't have to yell."

"Apparently I do!" she retorted at full volume, drawing dirty looks from several people. "Chat rooms are for sickos. Perverts, voyeurs, psychos—that's who hangs out in them."

"Shhhh," I growled back. Then through clenched teeth I added, "You're exaggerating."

But Janice didn't get the message. She ripped into me again, louder than ever. "That just shows how much you know. Or should I say how much you *don't* know? While you gullible little innocents are blabbing your faces off online, the crazies lurk in the background, taking it all in. Then when you least expect it, they pounce, and it's lambs to the slaughter."

I shook my head. "It isn't that kind of

chat room. It's on the school's website! Jeez. Do you really think the teachers and the parent council would give it the okay if it wasn't perfectly safe? You heard Marc Solomon. It's only open to Wellington students."

Janice let out a huge snort. "So flippin' what? You think there are no perverts at this school? Get real, Linda. Look around!"

"Yeah, like right beside you," a guy behind us sneered. "They don't come any more perverted than Beastly."

Right away Janice whirled on the guy, and I had to do a quick sidestep to keep from becoming a sandwich.

"How would you like your face rearranged?" she snarled, puffing up with anger.

Janice is a pretty big girl, but the guy didn't even flinch. In fact, he smiled. "You might want to look in the mirror, Beastly," he drawled. "Seems to me you're the one whose face could use some rearranging."

Encouraged by the grins and snickers of the kids around us, he added, "Have you ever considered plastic surgery? Or a paper bag maybe?"

Instant laughter from the crowd.

Instant blood boil from Janice. She lunged at the guy, but he was ready for her.

If you ask me, he was hoping she'd attack him. Janice's short fuse isn't exactly a secret, and with the way he was baiting her, he had to know it was just a matter of time before she lost her cool.

He didn't actually hit her. It was more like she ran into his hand—at least that's what everybody told the teacher who came to break things up. But I'm not so sure. Seems to me the guy's fist had to have had some force behind it to make Janice double over the way she did. It served him right when she barfed all over his shoes.

On the bright side, Janice and I suddenly had a clear path out of the gym. I wasn't crazy about being in the spotlight—it was kind of like riding on the main float of the Santa Claus parade. But, since Janice's aroma had people holding their noses and turning away, I hoped they wouldn't notice me trailing behind.

"Are you okay?" I asked, standing uselessly beside her in the washroom while she splashed water on her face and the floor.

"Yeah. I'm just dandy," she retorted sarcastically. "I love throwing up at this time of day. It gives me more room for lunch."

I didn't say anything. Even though Janice had sort of brought the situation on herself, I felt a little sorry for her. Guys aren't supposed to hit girls. It's an unwritten rule. Janice might not look like your usual girl and she certainly didn't act like your usual girl. That didn't mean she didn't feel like a girl inside.

"The guy is a jerk," she muttered. "Exactly the type of moron you're going to hook up with in a chat room." Then she wiped her face with a paper towel and stalked out of the washroom.

I have to admit I didn't completely disagree with her. I had my doubts about chat rooms too. I'd never visited one, so I didn't have any firsthand knowledge, but I'd heard a lot of horror stories. Computers getting hacked or infected with viruses. Kids getting sucked into cults. Some of the stuff was pretty scary.

But I wasn't going to admit that to Janice. She'd just think she'd talked some sense into me and let me know it with a great big *I told you so*. Well, thanks but no thanks. Janice Beasley could be as pushy as she liked; I was not going to let her do my thinking for me. I might visit the school's chat room or I might not. I hadn't decided yet. But that was the whole point. It was *my* decision.

I'm not really a big computer person. I have an e-mail address, but, except for the occasional joke from my cousin in California, the only messages I get are advertisements for pre-approved mortgages and cheap meds. I use the Internet if I need to research an assignment for school, but that's pretty much it.

That night though, I sat down at the computer right after supper. I still hadn't decided about the chat room, but I was tossing the pros and cons around in my head.

While I thought about it, I decided to check my e-mail. There were three new messages. The first was from the president of some war-torn African country. He wanted me to look after his money for him. I was flattered that he put so much trust in me considering we'd never even met. But I didn't need the responsibility. Delete. The second e-mail was from a lottery, notifying me that I'd just won two million dollars. It was a nice thought, but I'd won that lottery before, and I still hadn't received the money. Delete.

The third message was from Janice. All it said was *"Don't be an idiot."*

I sighed and shook my head. I should have known Janice wasn't finished ragging on me. She was just trying a different approach. I could almost see the determination on her face as she pounded the computer keys.

Well, too bad. I could be stubborn too.

Delete.

"B-bye, Janice." I smiled as the message vanished into cyberspace. Then without a second's hesitation, I clicked on *Google* and typed *Wellington High School home page* into the search window.

chapter three

Right away a photograph of the school popped up onto the screen. It was Wellington High all right, but not really. The orange brick walls climbed two stories just like always, but they were missing their usual graffiti. At the main entrance there were flowers instead of cigarette butts. The silver flagpole out front was the same, but the normally limp Canadian flag at the top looked like it had been starched. It was snapping in the breeze against a brilliant blue sky.

The picture was so perfect it could have been a postcard. I imagined myself filling out the back and sending it to my cousin. "Having a wonderful time—wish you were here."

It suddenly struck me that in all the months I'd been at Wellington, I'd never visited the school's website—not even once. So I spent the next few minutes checking out what was there.

It was pretty basic. There was a history of the school, a map of the building, a code of behavior, a calendar of events and a staff directory complete with e-mail addresses.

There was a link to the school board office and even a page where teachers could post assignments. Yeah right, like kids were going to check to see if they had homework.

Right below the photograph of the school, there was an icon that looked like a big sun. It was pulsing red and yellow, and in the middle of it, also pulsing, were bold, black letters that said *New!! Student Forum*.

I started to snigger. Student forum? It sounded so intellectual. Was the fancy title supposed to improve the quality of online chats or was it meant to pacify parents?

I clicked on the link, and the screen changed into a big rectangle divided into about sixteen cells of pictures—photographs of kids doing all kinds of school activities. I didn't recognize anyone in the pictures. That's because they weren't actually Wellington students. They were models pretending to be students. One by one, the pictures started to flip, until they were totally gone and replaced with the heading, Wellington High School—Student Forum.

Below the heading, in the bottom right-hand corner, were three subheadings—*Rules, Registering* and *Forums*.

Holding my breath, I clicked on the *Forums* link.

I don't know what I expected—maybe sirens and a flashing screen notifying the world that I was on the page—but of course that didn't happen. No one knew I was there. How could they know? I hadn't registered. And as long as I didn't, I was anonymous. I started to breathe again.

There were cartoon icons for each chat room and a menu that showed who was logged on. Nervously, I pulled down the menu for the *Homework Help* room. If my computer left some kind of electronic trail, at least my parents would be impressed with my wholesome choice. There were just three kids inside—Dash, Henny and Plato.

I wondered who they were in real life. Geeks no doubt. Who else would think about homework on a Friday night?

Next I checked out the menu for the *Wellington Room*. That was where kids could talk about what was going on at school. I couldn't believe my eyes. There had to be thirty names on the list!

I tried to imagine who they belonged to. Trixie, Zelda, Fish, 3M—most of the names were pretty weird. Mountain Man, Luster, Goddess, Freaky Filly—there was no way to tell who was who. What kind of kids would go to that room? Student council? School club members? Newspaper and yearbook reporters maybe?

I scanned the rest of the list, nervous and curious at the same time. Then one name caught my attention and I stopped. It was Cyrano—as in Cyrano de Bergerac. Only last week that movie had been on television. It was set in olden times. Once I got used to the guys in balloon pants and big floppy hats, I'd loved it! It was sad, but so romantic.

In the movie, Cyrano was in love with this beautiful girl named Roxane, but she didn't know he was alive. So when Cyrano's friend, Christian, asked Cyrano to help *him* win Roxane's heart, Cyrano wrote a bunch of amazing love letters and poems for Christian to give her. Now *that* is what I call true love.

What sort of teenage boy would choose Cyrano for a nickname? Most high school guys wouldn't have a clue who Cyrano de Bergerac was, so I was pretty sure it had to be someone who'd seen the movie. It also had to be someone sensitive and romantic.

Just the same, I was curious. I needed to know what Cyrano was saying. And that meant I had to go into the chat room.

Before I could change my mind, I clicked on the registration page. Psyching myself up for what I was about to do, I read the instructions seven or eight times. Then, flexing my fingers, I filled in the first information box with my student number. Moving to the second box, I typed in my e-mail address. There was just one more piece of information left to fill in—my nickname.

I didn't allow myself to think about what I was doing, because if I did, I knew I would chicken out. I just typed the name and hit Enter.

Zhwuuup! In a flash my information was gone, launched into cyberspace somewhere. Before I had time to blink, a new page appeared on the screen. It was bare except for two short sentences: *You are logged on, Roxane. You may now enter a forum.*

My heart started beating so hard it hurt. Oh my god—what had I done? I was a registered chatter! Now I could be traced. The site administrator could track me down.

So what? a voice inside my head demanded. You haven't done anything wrong. Everyone else can be traced too. That's what makes the chat rooms safe.

It was true. The site was safe. I had nothing to worry about. And besides, I had no intention of actually chatting. I just wanted to see what people talked about—especially Cyrano.

I navigated back to the Forums page and pulled down the menu for the *Wellington Room.* Cyrano was still there. Pressing my lips tightly together, I ran the cursor over the Enter button and left-clicked.

I was in.

The inside of the chat room was two pages rolled together—one on top of the other. The upper page framed the one underneath. It had a banner at the top identifying the chat room and a script box at the bottom where you could type what you wanted to say. As soon as you hit the Enter button, your message appeared on the page inside the frame along with the messages everyone else was sending.

Even though the chat room had only been open for a few hours, the list of messages was super long. Feeling like an eavesdropper I scrolled through the page, stopping now and then to read what people had written.

Lotto: This is 1 of the best ideas Wellington has ever had. 3 cheers for that kid who set it up.

Wingding: No kidding. Anybody

know when the next school dance is?

I scrolled down some more.

Ferris: If you're not in any of the events 4 the gym riot, do U have 2 go 2 school next Friday?

It was Cyrano who answered.

Cyrano: Why wouldn't U want 2 go? The gym riot's going 2 be great. Get involved. You'll have a lot of fun.

Something like relief washed over me. This Cyrano seemed just as nice as the one in the movie.

chapter four

My eyes were burning. No, that's not true. They were past burning. They'd moved on to aching, and they were watering too.

I turned off the computer and squinted at my watch. It was nearly ten o'clock! No wonder my eyes were killing me. I'd been staring at the computer screen for five straight hours.

"Linda?" My mother poked her head

around the door. "You still in here?" She sounded surprised. "Your dad and I have hardly seen you all weekend. Aren't you finished your homework *yet*?"

I glanced at the pile of schoolbooks on the corner of the desk and cringed. I hadn't even looked at my homework. I'd been so caught up in the school's chat rooms I'd completely forgotten I had any. And now that my eyes had gone on strike, I couldn't do homework if I wanted to.

I wasn't going to tell my mother that though.

"I was just going to bed," I said.

She gave my shoulder a squeeze. "Good. Enough is enough. Weekends are supposed to be a time to rest up and recharge your batteries. A little homework is fine, but this is ridiculous. I have half a mind to call the school and complain."

Instant panic.

"Ah, Mom," I groaned. "Don't do that. It'll just get my teachers ticked. And anyway, it's not like it happens all the time."

She didn't look convinced.

"I'm serious," I said. "I'm in high school, Mother. If you call the school, I'll look like a total loser."

She rolled her eyes and sighed. "Fine. I get the message. But this better not become a habit."

My heart started beating again. Now all I had to do was pray that none of my teachers collected the weekend's assignments.

I scooped up my books, gave Mom a peck on the cheek and headed for my room. I felt kind of guilty. I hadn't exactly lied to my mother, but if she knew I'd spent the entire weekend inside a chat room, she'd freak out.

Assuming she actually believed that's what I'd done, that is. Even I thought it was bizarre. All I'd intended to do was take a quick look to see if Cyrano was anything like the guy in the movie. That's it. Nothing more. But once I got inside and started reading all the messages, I couldn't stop.

By the end of the weekend I'd begun to feel like I knew the people who were writing them—the repeat chatters anyway.

There were lots of names that only showed up once—they were just checking things out I guess. There was also a bunch of kids who chatted everyday. After a while I got so I didn't even have to look to see who they were. I knew who was talking just by what they were saying and the abbreviations they used.

When I got to school Monday morning, I found myself secretly watching everyone I passed in the hall. Who was Fish? Who was 3M? And of course, who was Cyrano?

"Linda!" A voice broke into my thoughts and I looked around to see a girl hurrying along the hall toward me. It was Sheri Owen, the junior captain of my house team, and she was waving a paper in the air. "Linda Copley?" she said as she skidded to a stop.

I nodded.

"Just the person I'm looking for," she grinned and stabbed a finger at the paper. "You haven't signed up for the gym riot yet, and we still have lots of spots to fill."

On the outside I didn't move a hair, but on the inside I was backing up big-time. The last thing I needed was to make a fool of myself in front of the whole school. "Oh, I don't know, Sheri," I hedged while I tried to think of a good excuse for not signing up.

But Sheri shook her head. "Don't bail on me, Linda. Our house needs you. We really want to win this thing."

I shook my head and smiled self-consciously. "Then you don't want me. I'm terrible at sports."

She waved away my protest. "If you're worried about messing up, don't even think about it. This isn't like real sports. These are goofy events. *Everybody* looks silly doing them. That's what makes it fun. What do you say? I'll sign you up for the chain-gang relay. There will be a whole crowd of kids out there, so you'll blend right in. And remember, it's a beach theme, so dig out your shades and flip-flops and the wildest summer shirt you can find."

Then before I could open my mouth to argue, she added my name to the list and hurried off to pounce on another unsuspecting victim.

Wonderful! Now I could spend the entire week worrying about Friday. Or I could simply decide to be sick that day. Or—I thought about what Cyrano had said—I could go and have fun. It looked like everybody else had fun doing it, but...

I glanced up to see Janice standing at her locker. She was frowning at me. I pretended I didn't see and started dialing in my combo.

"What was that all about?" She nodded toward Sheri who was flitting from one kid to another like a crazed hummingbird.

I sighed. "She is recruiting for the gym riot."

"You didn't get sucked in, did you?"

I started to bristle. "Why do you have to be so negative about everything?"

"You did get sucked in," Janice snorted, turning back to her own locker.

"I did *not*!"

She eyed me skeptically. "You didn't sign up for an event?"

"So what if I did? Taking part in the world doesn't mean you've been sucked in. It means..." I scrambled for something profound to say. "It means you're taking part in the world." Then because I knew how lame that sounded, I snapped, "You should try it sometime."

Janice didn't seem impressed. Instead she changed the subject. "Did you get my e-mail?"

Oh, good. Something else for her to get on my case about. As I reached into my locker and started rooting around for my books, I muttered, "What e-mail?"

"Don't be cute. You know what e-mail I'm talking about. You've been chatting online, haven't you?"

I pulled my head out of my locker and glared at her. "For your information, I have *not* been chatting." Literally speaking, it was the truth. "Not that it's any of your business," I added. "And not that there's anything wrong with it either."

For about half a second, Janice seemed surprised. But then her expression became smug again and she said, "Oh, I get it. You've been *into* the chat rooms. You just haven't done any talking yet."

What could I say? She was right. I sure as heck wasn't going to admit that to her though. So I just shut my locker door and left.

chapter five

It really bugged me the way Janice lectured me whenever I didn't agree with her. If she was entitled to think what she wanted, then so was I. And I could do what I wanted too. But there was no sense living through one of her tirades if I didn't have to. So when I went from being a chat room observer to becoming an actual participant, I didn't bother telling her.

It was Tuesday evening, and I had just logged into *The Hot Spot*. The topic was music, and people were trying to figure out what the top-selling album of all time was.

Frisky Filly: I bet it's rap. Something by Eminem.

3M: Nah. Doubt it. It's gotta be an album from a million years ago.

Wingding: Something by The Rolling Stones? Those guys have been around 4ever.

3M: Why not something modern like Usher's Confessions? That's really big.

Wingding: Usher sucks. Maybe he's hot now, but he won't be 4 long.

3M: So what? The CD will still have sold a lot.

Dogger: It could be a movie soundtrack. My sister works in a music store, and she says soundtracks are really big.

Frisky Filly: My money's on *Thriller* by Michael Jackson. My parents say it was huge in the '80s.

Roxane: You're close. *Thriller* is #2. The Eagles Greatest Hits has it beat. I saw it on Much Music.

I pulled my fingers back from the keyboard as if it had burned me. I couldn't believe what I'd just done.

Surfing through the chat rooms during the last five days I'd been like a fly on the wall, quietly taking everything in. It had felt weird at first, like I was eavesdropping or something, but after a while I'd stopped thinking about it.

I just wanted to see what everyone had to say. I never planned to get involved, though, and now I felt totally exposed.

Staring at the monitor, I waited for one

of the other chatters to shoot me down. Then Cyrano's name popped up on the screen, and I felt my whole body clench. But when I read what he said, I relaxed again.

Cyrano: That's right. I saw that Much Music show too. 28 mill. That's how many *Greatest Hits* albums The Eagles have sold. *Thriller* sold 27.

Anxiously I waited for the next few messages, expecting someone to challenge or belittle what I'd said. But it didn't happen. Nobody treated my comments any differently than anyone else's.

I know it sounds dumb, but that was a major turning point for me. For the rest of the week, I visited the chat rooms every day and took part in the conversations. It was the first time I had ever been part of a group. It didn't matter who the chat room people were in real life. The important thing was that while we were online, I was one of them.

I was happier than I'd been in my entire school life. Don't get me wrong. I'm not saying I'm normally an unhappy person. I'm not. It's just that I felt bouncier, kind of like I was walking on a trampoline.

Everything seemed easier, even breathing, and no matter what happened during the day, I knew I had something to look forward to when I got home. I didn't even worry about the gym riot coming up on Friday.

Until it arrived, that is.

As I started getting into my beach clothes, all my insecurities resurfaced. Was everyone going to think I looked dumb? What if I messed up during my event? Were people going to laugh at me? And what if my house lost because I screwed up?

I studied my reflection in the mirror— white capris, floral Hawaiian shirt, ponytail sticking out the back of a Blue Jays ball cap, sunglasses, sunscreen on my nose and turquoise flip-flops on my feet.

I definitely looked summery, but what if all the other girls looked like swimsuit models?

I couldn't take the chance. I whipped off the beach outfit and replaced it with a pair of black shorts and a plain white T-shirt. Then I put on my socks and runners. I looked at myself again. Now I was pretty much invisible, but at least I wouldn't get laughed at.

I still felt like I was dressed in neon lights when I took the floor for the chain-gang relay. I knew Janice was sitting in the bleachers somewhere, shaking her head at my stupidity, but I didn't look around to see where she was. Instead I let my eyes glaze over, pasted a smile on my face and tried to look like I fit in.

Sheri was right about lots of people taking part in the event. There were four teams and a dozen kids on each team. I didn't know many of the grade tens, elevens and twelves, but I'd spent my entire school life with most of the grade nines, so I searched for a familiar face.

Chad Sharp, the guy who'd started the chat rooms, was on my team. He looked as self-conscious as I felt, so I went and stood beside him.

Right away, he looked relieved. Misery loves company, I guess.

"Sheri got you too?" he mumbled, his face instantly flushing bright red.

I shrugged. "Maybe it'll be fun." I'm not sure who I was trying to convince, Chad or myself.

And then someone from the student council was at the microphone explaining the rules. The chain-gang relay was an obstacle course that you had to complete holding hands, so that each team formed a human chain. If you broke the chain you had to start over. The first team to finish was the winner.

Sandy Wade from my English class grabbed one of my hands and dragged me into line. Then somebody else took my other hand and fell in behind me. The hand was hot and sweaty, and I glanced back to see who it belonged to. It was

Chad. He looked more uncomfortable than ever, so I smiled.

And then we were off. At first all I noticed were the screaming spectators, but as we got deeper into the race, their shouts faded away, and I focused on clearing the obstacles and hanging on to Sandy and Chad. No fear there: Sandy's nails dug into my hand like hooks, and Chad had hold of me so tight, I couldn't have shaken him loose if I'd tried.

Our team messed up twice, but I guess the other teams had to start over too, because somehow we won.

And then suddenly I could hear the crowd again. Everybody was cheering. It was great—except for one thing. My left hand felt as if the bones in it had been welded together.

"Chad," I winced as I tried to pry my crushed fingers free. "If you're finished with my hand, do you think I could have it back?"

chapter six

After school I couldn't wait to visit the chat rooms, but if I headed for the computer the second I walked in the door, my parents would wonder what was going on. Luckily they had a party to go to that night, so as soon as they left I logged into the *Wellington Room*.

I hadn't expected many kids to be online—after all, it was Friday night—but there were quite a few chatters. They were all talking about the gym riot. It had been a huge success. Reliving it made it even better, and after reading everyone's comments I started to feel like I'd had a good time too.

Fish: That bat-spinning race was hilarious. I swear I peed myself laughing.

Roxane: I wondered what that puddle on the floor was.

Cyrano: Ooh, good 1. She got ya, man.

Somewhere around ten o'clock, the chatters started dropping out, and by eleven, the only ones left were Cyrano and me. We were still rehashing the day.

Cyrano: So what was your favorite event?

Roxane: I liked the blindfolded feeding contest. That was pretty funny. And messy! I also liked the chain-gang relay. What about U?

Cyrano: What a coincidence!!! Those were my fave events 2!! Great minds think alike.

Roxane: Or small minds seldom differ.

Cyrano: I think U just insulted me.

Oh, no! I hammered on the Delete key and swore at myself. *Dummy, dummy, dummy*! Cyrano and I had been having such a great conversation, and now I'd gone and ruined it by insulting him. What an idiot I was!

My hands shook as I placed them back on the keyboard.

Roxane: Sorry, Cyrano. No offense intended. At my house, it's a saying.

I forced myself to stop writing. Groveling

would only make matters worse. I hit Enter and held my breath as I waited for Cyrano's reply.

It felt like I sat there forever, but it couldn't have been more than a minute before the screen reloaded with his answer.

Cyrano: I was kidding!! We have the same saying at my house. Besides, if U were insulting me, U were insulting yourself 2.

I was so relieved, I laughed out loud. With my lighthearted mood restored, I sent back a smart aleck comment.

Roxane: U figured that out, did ya?

Cyrano: Ho-ho! The girl has got attitude!

That's when I heard Mom and Dad coming through the front door. *Darn*! I couldn't let them find me in a chat room.

Why did they have to show up right when I was having a good time? Reluctantly I put my hands back on the keyboard and prepared to log off.

Roxane: And she also has 2 get off the computer. But it's been fun talking 2 U.

Cyrano: Ditto. So how about we do it again? Say Sunday afternoon? Same chat room?

Roxane: Sounds good. Talk 2 U then. Bye.

I grinned all the way to my room. *I had a date*! Well, sort of a date. The closest I'd ever come to having a date, anyway.

I'm fifteen years old, in grade nine, and nobody's ever asked me out. I've never even danced with a boy! I know I'm not a goddess or anything, but I'm not paper bag ugly either. And I dress okay. I don't have bad breath or B.O. I do normal teenager stuff. But I've never had a date.

I started grinning again. That was about to change.

I was still smiling when I climbed into bed.

"Stop it, Linda!" I scolded myself.

Even if hooking up with Cyrano on Sunday *was* a date, it wasn't me who was having it. It was Roxane. If Cyrano knew I was Roxane, he wouldn't be the least bit interested.

Maybe it was the name he liked. Roxane certainly sounded zippier than Linda. I wasn't named after anybody, so I have no idea why my parents couldn't have chosen something more original. Why not Lindi or Linley? Even a different spelling—say, Lynda—would have been better.

What kind of a chance did I have against the Caitlyns, Mirandas and Bethanys of the world with a boring name like Linda?

I resisted visiting any of the chat rooms again until Sunday. For one thing I didn't want my parents asking me why I was on the computer so much lately. Also I wanted the Sunday chat with Cyrano to be special.

We wouldn't be the only ones in the chat room, of course, but that didn't change the fact that he'd specially asked me to be there.

At one o'clock I went to the school website and pulled down the *Wellington Room* menu to see who was inside. There were a half-dozen kids, but Cyrano wasn't one of them. At two o'clock I checked again. And then at two-fifteen. At two-thirty he was there. But I didn't want to seem too anxious, so I didn't log on for another ten minutes.

The topic this time was Monday's big basketball game against Creighton High. The Warriors had beaten us in last year's city final, so this was a big grudge match.

Fish: The Warriors don't stand a

chance. They've lost 3 of their starters from last season.

Kingpin: We've lost players 2. Sabourin and Willows are gone—they were our big scorers.

Fish: Yeah, but we picked up a couple of really good players like that new kid from Calgary. I forget his name— he can shoot the lights out.

3M: Our rookies aren't 2 shabby. I bet we can beat Creighton EZ.

Cyrano: I think we'll win 2, but it isn't going 2 B a piece of cake. The Warriors are a good team. And they have amazing fans. They get more kids out 2 their away games than a lot of schools get at home. We can't let them have that advantage. We have 2 fill the gym with our own fans. So tomorrow remind everyone 2 go 2 the game and cheer their faces off.

Frisky Filly: Holy cheerleader, Batman!
R U a fan or what!

Cyrano: U bet. I never miss a game.
The team can't lose when I wear my
lucky Wellington Tigers shirt. Those
black and orange stripes paralyze the
opposition.

I reread Cyrano's message. He was
going to be at tomorrow's basketball
game—a spectator, not a player. And he
was going to be wearing an orange and
black striped shirt. If I wanted to find
out who he was in real life, all I had to
do was go to the game.

My heart did a flip. Had Cyrano
dropped those clues on purpose? Did he
want me to know who he was? Did he
want to know who I was too?

It was time to let him know I was in
the chat room.

Roxane: Lucky shirt, huh? Whatever
works for ya, I guess.

Cyrano: Hey, Roxie. I wondered if you were going 2 log on 2day. Going 2 the big game 2morrow?

I hadn't planned on it, but now it was definitely on my agenda.

Roxane: Absolutely.

Cyrano: Good. Make sure U wear your striped shirt.

I only hesitated a second before typing my response.

Roxane: I'm not really the striped shirt type. I think I'll stick with my lucky stuffed Wellington Tiger.

Cyrano: Like U said—whatever works.

chapter seven

I don't think I closed my eyes that night.
There was no point. I couldn't have slept
if I'd tried. There was too much going on
in my head. I was arguing with myself so
much I was beginning to wonder if I had
a multiple personality disorder.

Part of me was bouncing off the
ceiling. Cyrano liked me. I'm not saying
he was in love with me or anything, but
he wanted to meet me in real life. Why

else would he have dropped all those clues?

He just got caught up in the school spirit thing and didn't think about what he was saying, said the sensible me. He probably didn't even realize he'd dropped any clues.

But he asked what I was going to wear to the game, the excited part of me insisted. Why would he do that unless he wanted to know who I was?

Then another voice—one that sounded a lot like Janice—piped up. If you show up at that game tomorrow carrying a stuffed tiger, you're asking for trouble. If you had half a brain, you wouldn't go anywhere near that gym.

I have to admit I *was* nervous about revealing my identity. I liked the Cyrano I knew online, but what if he wasn't like that in real life? He was smart and funny in the chat rooms, but what if he turned out to be a loser—a loser who thought I liked him? Then I'd really have a problem.

On the other hand, he might be absolutely awesome in person and be totally disappointed in who *I* was. If that happened, I'd never be able to show my face at school again.

When morning finally rolled around, I still didn't know what I was going to do. Maybe I'd go to the game. Maybe I wouldn't. But just in case, I spent extra time on my hair and makeup.

I also made a trip to my old toy chest in the basement and dug out a small plush stuffy, an orange cat that used to sit on my bed. It didn't have any stripes, but a black felt marker took care of that.

"Coming to the game?" I asked Janice as we headed to our lockers after school.

She rolled her eyes. "As if. Are you?"

I shrugged. "I thought I might. It's a really big game, you know. Creighton beat us out for the championship last year. This is our chance for revenge. Why don't you come? It'll be fun." The truth of the matter was I didn't want to go alone.

Janice eyed me skeptically. "Since when are you a basketball fan?"

"I'm not, not really." There was no sense trying to lie. I'd never pull it off.

"Why are you going to the game then?"

"Everybody is."

"Who is everybody?"

I heaved an exasperated sigh. "Everybody! You know—the kids in school. People with school spirit. What do you want, *names*?"

Janice crossed her arms and flopped against her locker. "Yeah," she drawled. "Give me some names."

"You're being stupid."

"You wish," she said. "You can't give me names because you don't have any. Not real names anyway. You're going to the game because all your little chat room buddies are going. Am I right?"

"What is wrong with you?" I growled.

Janice shook her head as if I was the most pathetic excuse for a human being she'd ever seen.

"Maybe you ought to look in the mirror when you ask that question," she said. And then she walked away.

She hadn't yelled or slammed her locker door. She hadn't even glared at me. She'd just said her piece and left. Maybe she'd given up trying to bully me and decided to use scare tactics instead.

Scared is exactly how I felt as I headed toward the gym. Everyone else was laughing and hurrying along the hallway like they were on their way to the event of a lifetime.

I, on the other hand, could have been walking to the gas chamber. At least ten times I lost my nerve, but my feet didn't get the message. They just kept right on walking.

The bleachers were already packed when I entered the gym. I tried to focus on faces to see if there was anyone I knew well enough to sit beside. But all I could make out was a solid mass of bodies.

The gym was vibrating with music and basketballs were pounding the floor as the teams went through their warm-ups. People were pushing me from behind, so I had no choice but to keep moving.

About halfway around the gym, I saw a group of girls five rows up. I didn't know any of them, but it didn't matter. There was an empty spot beside them on the end of the bleacher. It wasn't huge, but then neither am I. I could squeeze into it.

Stepping over and around the bodies on the rows below, I climbed up and claimed the seat. The girl I parked beside sent me a snotty look, but at least she didn't hip check me off the bleacher.

I pulled the tiger stuffy out of my schoolbag and set it on my lap. Then I started looking around the gym for an orange and black striped shirt. Right away my hopes tumbled into my shoes. A third of the guys in the gym were wearing orange and black striped shirts!

Somebody must have given out the school's rugby and soccer jerseys. Had Cyrano known that was going to happen? Had I been set up?

I felt so stupid!

"Hi," said a voice beside the bleacher.

"What?" Startled, I glanced down to see Chad Sharp looking at me. "Oh, hi," I replied, sticking a smile on top of the frown I was wearing. I can only imagine what that must have looked like.

"Do you mind if I stand here?" he mumbled into his chest. "There are no seats left."

I peered around the gym. A lot of people were standing. "I must've gotten the last one," I said, hoping I sounded more cheerful than I felt.

He nodded toward the players taking their positions on the floor. "You a fan?"

"Oh, yeah." I gave my stuffed tiger a spin in the air. "Woo-hoo. Go Wellington!"

And then the whistle blew, the referee threw the ball up in the air and the game was underway. My eyes followed the players up and down the floor, and I clapped every time the Tigers scored, but my mind was not on the game. Janice was right. I shouldn't have come. Out of the corner of my eye I could see Chad. There was nothing I wanted more than to tear out of that gym, but I couldn't leave with him standing there. Like it or not, I was trapped.

If I'd really been a fan, I guess that wouldn't have been so bad. Everybody else seemed to be enjoying the game. They were certainly making enough noise. The only time it ever got quiet was when our guys were shooting free throws.

So, of course, that's when it happened. The score was tied, and our team was at the line. You could feel the tension in the air. And then, just as the shooter went to release the ball, the girl beside me grabbed the little stuffy out of my lap. She started jumping up and down and waving it in the air. "Go Tigers! Go Tigers!"

Every head in the gym turned to look at her—at her and my tiger.

chapter eight

When the girl went to give me back my stuffy, I told her to keep it. What did it matter now? Everyone in the gym had seen her waving it around. Including Cyrano. No doubt he thought she was Roxane.

This was not how things were supposed to work out. Cyrano was supposed to wear a striped shirt, and I was supposed to pick him out of the crowd. Then when I waved my little stuffed tiger, he was supposed to pick *me* out of the crowd. After that we would start talking. Things would go from there. It might not be Cinderella and Prince Charming but it was a start.

Yeah, right! Some start. I was no closer to knowing who Cyrano was than I had been a week ago. And he didn't know who I was either.

Even worse, he thought I was somebody else. Okay, maybe he didn't think *I* was somebody else, but he thought Roxane was! The situation was about as messed up as it could get.

I didn't visit the chat rooms that night. I couldn't. Now that Cyrano had a face for Roxane, he was either going to be turned off or turned on. Either way, it was bad news for me.

If he didn't like the look of the girl waving my toy tiger, he might ignore me in the chat room. But if he did talk to me, he would think he was talking to her. Confused identities were so romantic in the movies, but in real life they were frustrating.

61

I was nervous about going to school the next day. At the moment the only one who knew about the mix-up was me, but it was only a matter of time until Cyrano figured it out. Eventually he would talk to that girl, and when he did he'd put all the pieces together. Then how stupid would I look?

In the meantime I had to keep Janice from finding out, and that was not going to be easy. Janice always seemed to know when I was hiding something, and she had a nasty habit of nagging me until I spilled the beans. It didn't usually take too long. Lying is another one of those things I'm not very good at.

I got to school early, hoping to get my books out of my locker and sneak into homeroom before Janice showed up. But—wouldn't you know it—she was already there. And from the look of it, she was waiting for me.

I took a deep breath and tried to look natural.

"You're here early," I said, focusing

my attention on my lock so she couldn't read my face.

"So are you," she replied.

"I forgot my homework last night, so I came in to do it before class," I lied.

"You sure?" she said.

I looked over and frowned at her. "What are you talking about? Of course I'm sure."

She shrugged. "I just thought maybe you'd snagged yourself a boyfriend and had an early morning date."

I was stunned. What hat had she pulled that out of? If I didn't know better, I would've said Janice knew what was going on. But she couldn't. I hadn't talked to her since yesterday at our lockers. More than likely she'd just made a lucky guess.

"Very funny," I scowled. "I don't have a boyfriend, and you know it."

Janice reached into her locker and pulled out a long triangular-shaped package. There was no mistaking what it was. I'd done the Mother's Day thing enough times to recognize florist's paper when I saw it.

"Well, if you're sure you don't have a boyfriend, then I guess the custodian must have left this," she shrugged. "Maybe it's a thank-you for keeping your locker tidy."

She held the package out to me. "It was on the floor when I got here." She pointed to a small white envelope taped to the wrapping paper. "It's addressed to you." Then she closed her locker and walked away.

I don't know how long I stood with my mouth hanging open, but when I went to call Janice back, she was gone. I looked down the hall both ways. It was empty. I was the only one around.

I didn't know what to do. I'd never received flowers before. Was I supposed to open the card first or the package?

I opted for the package. There was no sense getting my hopes up for nothing. More than likely, Janice was playing a joke on me and had wrapped up weeds or something.

The paper came away without a fight, and inside, much to my surprise, was a gorgeous, long-stemmed rose. It wasn't dead or anything. In fact, it was in a vial of water, and there was a stem of baby's breath with it.

I touched the yellow petals. They were velvety soft. I put my face close to them and breathed deeply. They smelled gorgeous.

But who was the rose from?

Cradling the package in my arm, I felt around the outside of the paper for the envelope and ripped it free. It was definitely addressed to me. I couldn't stand the suspense any longer. I tore open the flap and pulled out the white card.

A flower to replace your tiger, it read, and it was signed, C.

I gasped. Then I started grinning like an idiot. C! It was signed, C! The rose was from Cyrano! He *had* spotted me at the game. And if the rose meant anything, he hadn't hated what he'd seen.

I couldn't wait to let Cyrano know how much I liked the rose. Actually it wasn't the rose I was thrilled with so much as what it stood for. It meant Cyrano knew who I was, and he was interested.

I went on the computer around eight o'clock. Cyrano wasn't in any of the chat rooms. I scanned through the day's postings, but his name didn't appear in any of them. He hadn't logged on yet.

I waited for an hour, but when he still hadn't shown up, I decided to leave a message—something that *he* would understand, but nobody else would.

I hopped from chat room to chat room, waiting for someone to bring up a topic that I could casually work my secret message into. It was Frisky Filly who provided the perfect opening. Kids were talking about the upcoming dance, and Filly wanted to know why guys never gave girls corsages anymore.

Frisky Filly: My grandma says guys always brought flowers 4 their dates.

This was my chance. I couldn't get my message typed fast enough.

Roxane: Sounds good 2 me. Bring back the good old days! I'd love 4 a guy 2 give me flowers, especially yellow roses.

Then I hit Enter, and as my message popped up on the screen, I heaved a satisfied sigh and sank back in my chair. That should do the trick nicely.

chapter nine

Janice never asked me who left the rose. In fact she never mentioned it at all. I was sort of disappointed. I mean, here I was floating around in the clouds—I couldn't have been higher if I'd been on drugs. I wanted to share my excitement with someone, even if that someone was Janice. The secret was just too delicious to keep to myself.

So when Cyrano's next gift arrived,

I didn't try to hide it. This time it was candy—a huge box of chocolates mailed to the school! I couldn't believe it when I got called to the office to pick it up. Of course Janice heard my name over the public address system, and when she asked me about it, I couldn't help myself. I started gushing about Cyrano.

I expected her to jump down my throat. But all she did was close her eyes and shake her head. She didn't say a word. She didn't even try a chocolate.

However, when the poem showed up, I kept it completely to myself. It was delivered through the vents of my locker, and it was much too personal to share with anyone.

The poem said things Cyrano could never say in a chat room. Even though I read it in the privacy of the girls' washroom, I still blushed.

Suddenly my life had turned into a wonderful dream.

Even so, I still found myself getting frustrated. I wanted the dream to become reality. Cyrano knew who I was, and I wanted to know who he was too. We continued to meet in the chat rooms, but now that our relationship had moved to another level, that wasn't enough for me.

In the chat rooms, we were never alone. There were always dozens of other chatters, and though I left subtle messages about his gifts, Cyrano never let on that he understood.

I guess he didn't want to make the other chatters suspicious, but that didn't help me. I needed some kind of acknowledgment. He obviously liked me. Why else would he give me presents? When was he going to show himself?

The answer to that question arrived on Friday, along with another gift. Like the poem, it arrived through the vents of my locker.

I found it as I was putting my books away after school. I picked it up and read the now familiar handwriting. *For Linda*. I assumed it was another poem, but when I tore open the envelope, tucked inside was a ticket to that night's dance. And stuck to the ticket was a Post-it telling me he'd meet me at the entrance to the gym at eight o'clock.

Janice must have heard me squeal, because right away she peered around the door of her locker. "What's the matter?"

"Nothing." I had my hand over my mouth to keep from blinding her with my smile.

She rolled her eyes. "Let me guess. Your secret admirer has struck again."

I nodded. "He wants me to go to the dance with him. Look." I held out the envelope. "He even bought me a ticket."

Suddenly Janice didn't seem bored anymore. "What? Let me see that." She snatched the ticket out of my hand. "You're not going, right?"

I grabbed the ticket back. "Don't be ridiculous. Of course I'm going. This is my chance to meet Cyrano face-to-face. Why wouldn't I do it?"

"Because you don't know anything about the guy. He could be a fruitcake."

"He is not a fruitcake. I've been talking with him practically every day for nearly three weeks. He's really nice."

She dismissed my comments with a sneer. "You don't know that. Anybody can pretend to be someone they're not when they're in a chat room. For all you know, *I* could be this Cyrano character."

I have to admit that shook me up a little.

"You aren't, though, are you?" I asked warily.

"Of course I'm not!" she bellowed. "Don't be an idiot. I wouldn't be caught dead in a chat room. I just don't want you to be caught dead *outside* one."

I screwed up my face. "What are you talking about?"

"Did it ever occur to you that you could get hurt? You don't know this guy! So you chat with him online. So he sends you presents. So what? He could still be a nutcase."

"He isn't."

"Says you. Can't you see what's

happening? You're so desperate to have a boyfriend you don't care who the guy is. You'd throw yourself into the arms of the Boston Strangler if he looked at you sideways!"

"Shut up, Janice." I don't normally say stuff like that, but this time Janice had pushed me too far. "I am really tired of listening to you and your negative attitude," I seethed. "It doesn't seem to bother you that everybody is having fun except you. You actually seem to like being on the outside of everything. Well, fine. If you want to hate the world, go right ahead. But count me out. I've finally got a chance to become a part of things, and I'm going to take it. Whether you approve or not, I'm going to this dance."

You would have thought I'd hit her. She actually fell back a couple of steps. But she didn't say a word. She just closed her locker and left. She didn't even say goodbye.

Janice and I normally ride the same bus home, but I didn't want to risk another argument, so I stalled until I knew the bus had left. Then I began walking.

The rain started when I was about halfway home. As soon as the first fat drops splatted the sidewalk I knew it was going to be a downpour. I walked faster. And then when the sky ripped open, I started to run. It didn't help; in less than a minute I was drenched.

A dark green car with its wipers going a mile a minute splashed up alongside the curb, and the passenger window slid down. The driver leaned across the seat. It was Marc Solomon.

"Get in," he hollered over the rain. "I'll give you a ride."

chapter ten

Wonderful! Here was a grade twelve guy—the student council president no less!—offering me a ride in his car, and I looked like I'd just gone over Niagara Falls without the barrel! If it had been possible, I would've slithered down the storm drain along with the rain.

With as much dignity as I could manage, I smiled wetly and shook my head. "Thanks, but I really don't mind walking."

"Don't be silly," he said. "It's pouring."

I squinted up at the rain. "Well, I couldn't get much wetter, and I don't want to wreck your car."

He pushed open the door. "It's just water. Come on. Get in."

I was all out of arguments, so I slid into the seat beside him. Actually, sopping wet jeans don't really slide. Basically I just plopped onto the seat and then seesawed from one butt cheek to the other until I was far enough inside to shut the door. Very glamorous. Then I proceeded to drip all over the leather upholstery. In a matter of seconds, I was sitting in a puddle.

"How come you're out in the rain?" he asked as he steered the car back into traffic.

"I missed my bus."

He nodded. "So where's home?"

"Right here. I've always lived in—" I

could feel my cheeks turning red. "Oh," I winced. "Oh. Oh, you mean what street do I live on!" I threw my hands up over my face. "Oh, gawd. I'm such an idiot!"

Marc laughed. "No, you're not. But I do need to know where to drop you off."

"The nearest bridge would be good," I muttered through my hands.

He laughed again. "That's pretty funny. You're definitely the queen of one-liners. I don't think many people know that."

I pulled my hands away from my face and looked at him curiously. "What do you mean?"

"Well, around school, you're pretty quiet. You don't let people see your goofy side."

I have to admit I was a bit confused. Until that moment, I had never spoken to Marc Solomon in my life. So how did he know I had a goofy side? "I guess I'm sort of a stay-in-the-background kind of a person," I said.

"Not online you're not, Roxane."

My head snapped up so fast it hurt. "What did you call me?"

"Roxane. That is your chat room name, isn't it?"

I frowned. "Yeah, but how do you...I don't under—" And then I felt my eyes bulging out of my head. "Are you saying you're..."

He nodded and his mouth split into a huge grin. "Cyrano's the name and chat room's my game."

"Oh, my gawd!" I gasped. "*You're* Cyrano?"

He nodded again.

Could this be true? Was my secret admirer Marc Solomon? "But you can't be," I said. "You're...you're...you're the student council president."

He started to laugh again. "Even the student council president has to have a chat room nickname." Then he pulled the car over to the side of the road and his expression turned serious. "You realize that I've just broken all the rules by telling you my online identity."

I nodded.

He sighed. "The truth is I've been arguing with myself about telling you ever since the basketball game. I was sitting right behind you on the bleachers, so I saw you with your lucky Wellington tiger. You mentioned it in the chat room." He shrugged.

"That's how I knew you were Roxane. Considering the great chats we've had online, it didn't seem fair that I knew who you were, but you didn't know who I was."

I nodded again, and then my heart did a total somersault as he leaned toward me and looked right into my eyes.

"But it's got to be our secret. Okay? If word got out, I'd lose all my credibility with the student body—*and* the teachers."

"I won't tell a soul," I said solemnly. "I swear."

"Good." His smile was back. "Now tell me where you live so I can drive you home."

The rest of the ride was a beautiful blur,

but much too short, and I found myself wishing I lived farther from the school.

As Marc pulled into my driveway, he said, "So are you coming to the dance?"

I patted my schoolbag and smiled shyly. "I have the ticket right here."

"Great," he said. "Then I'll see you tonight."

I told my parents I was going to the mall. It was a lie, but it was easier than saying I was going to the dance. Considering I'd never been to a dance, my mother would have flipped into "twitter" mode.

She would have wanted to know who I was going with, who was going to be there, what I was going to wear, how I was going to do my hair, etc., etc. And then when I got home she'd be waiting at the door for a play-by-play of the evening. I was not ready for that.

My stomach was doing gymnastics when the bus pulled up beside the school. The rain had stopped, but there were still pond-sized puddles all over the place. As

I started across the parking lot I stepped right into the middle of one.

Instantly muddy water flooded my shoe and splashed onto my pants. It was enough to make me want to jump back onto the bus and go home. But the image of Marc Solomon waiting inside kept me from bolting, and I continued squishing my way toward the school.

With each step I became more and more nervous. Why was I putting myself through this? I was no good in crowds, and that's what dances were. Besides, I wasn't a great dancer. And who went to a dance alone, anyway?

You won't be alone, I reminded myself. Once I got inside Marc would be there, and then everything would be great. I felt inside my pocket for my ticket and kept walking.

The music had been loud in the parking lot, but once I stepped through the front door of the school, it was deafening.

My heart started to race, and I immediately began scanning the hallway for Marc. There were clumps of kids everywhere. I searched each group for his face. But he wasn't there.

Thinking he must already be inside, I started toward the gym. The guy and girl manning the ticket table were laughing with the kids waiting to go inside. While the girl took their tickets, the guy stamped their hands.

I fell into line and peered into the blackness of the gym. Marc had said he'd meet me at the entrance at eight o'clock. I looked at my watch. It was three minutes past.

What if he didn't show up? What if he forgot about me? He was the student council president. He probably had all kinds of jobs to do at the dance. Even if he did show up, he couldn't spend every minute with me.

My stomach started to churn. Then what? I didn't belong to any group, and I couldn't just start talking to people. Was I supposed to stand in a corner all night?

"Do you have a ticket?" a voice broke into my thoughts.

"Pardon?" I looked down at the girl at the table. How had I gotten to the front of the line so fast?

"Do you have a ticket?" she repeated patiently and nodded toward the gym. "For the dance?"

"Uh, yeah. Yeah, I do." Feeling flustered and stupid, I reached into my pocket, and as I slid the ticket across the table, I looked into the gym again. There was still no sign of Marc.

And that's when I knew there wasn't going to be. The happy little fog I'd been walking around in suddenly evaporated.

I felt like I was seeing clearly for the first time in weeks. A grade twelve guy wasn't going to be interested in a teeny-bop grade niner like me. This was all just a joke, and the laugh was on me.

The guy was ready to stamp my hand, but I pulled it away.

"If you leave the dance you have to have a stamp to get back in," he said.

I shook my head. "That's okay. I...I'm not going in. I've changed my mind."

The expression on the girl's face clearly said she thought I was a nutcase. Maybe I was. But at that point I didn't care. I just wanted to get out of there before I embarrassed myself even more.

I ran for the exit and leaned into the door just as someone on the other side yanked it open. Unable to stop myself, I flew into the night, straight toward the pavement.

chapter eleven

I gritted my teeth and prepared to fall on my face.

But it didn't happen. Somewhere between lunge and splat, somebody grabbed onto me and broke my fall. I still did a crazy spinout, but I managed to stay on my feet.

"Are you okay?" the person holding me up asked. It was Chad Sharp.

Kristin Butcher

Sorting out my arms and legs, I shrugged sheepishly. "Aside from feeling like a complete fool, yeah, I'm fine."

"Sorry about that," he mumbled. "I didn't see you on the other side of the door."

I shrugged again. "It's not your fault. I should've been watching where I was going."

"Where *are* you going?" Chad said and then quickly added, "If you don't mind me asking. The dance isn't over yet, is it?"

It was a pathetic attempt at humor, but all I said was, "It is for me."

"But it's only eight o'clock."

I sighed and started walking toward the parking lot. "It's a long story—and not very interesting. But thanks for saving me from the sidewalk."

"Wait. Do you have a ride? Do you want me to walk with you?"

"Don't be silly," I shooed him away. "I'll just grab the next bus. Go to the dance. I'm perfectly fine." And then I stepped into my second puddle of the night. "*Damn it, damn it, damn it!*" I hollered, stomping my foot in frustration. The water sprayed up like a fountain. Now I was wet all the way up to my knees.

"You're upset," Chad said.

I whirled on him. "Ya think?"

He pulled back. "I don't just mean about the puddle. You were upset before you left the school."

"Of course I was upset!" I blurted. "I just got stood up!"

Wonderful! Now I was sharing my life's story with a guy I hardly knew. "Sorry," I apologized. "I shouldn't be taking my troubles out on you. Good night." And I continued across the parking lot.

But Chad didn't get the message. He stuck to my side like a devoted dog. I started walking faster. He sped up too. Finally he grabbed my wrist and pulled me to a stop.

"Excuse me?" I scowled at him. "What do you think you're doing?"

He dropped his hand. "You didn't."

I had no idea what he was talking about. "I didn't what?"

"You didn't get stood up. Tonight, at the dance, you didn't get stood up."

I rolled my eyes. "Right. And you would know this *how*?"

The corners of his mouth twitched. "Because I'm your date and I'm right here."

Now I was completely baffled. "You aren't making any sense."

"I'm your date. I'm the one who sent you the ticket for the dance."

I stopped walking. How did Chad know about that? Slowly I shook my head. "No, you're not. You couldn't be."

"And the chocolates, and the poem, and the rose too," he said. "All from me."

Something between disbelief and horror wedged itself behind my ribs, making it hard to breath. "No. No, you're lying. You're not Cyrano."

"I never said I was."

"But it was Cyrano who sent me all those things. He even signed them!"

"*I* signed them. With a C—for Chad. I know you thought they were from Cyrano.

I could tell from the messages you posted in the chat rooms. But they were from me."

"I don't believe you." The truth was I didn't want to believe him. I wanted Cyrano—Mark—to be my secret admirer.

"I can recite the poem if you like."

"No!" I knew every line of that poem by heart, and Chad was not the person I imagined saying it.

How could this be happening? Suddenly my world was upside down.

"Don't be mad," he said. "I've liked you for a long time. Even before I knew you were Roxane."

I gasped. "How do you know about *that*?"

"The tiger at the basketball game. You told everyone in the chat room you'd be carrying it."

That was true, but I'd only wanted Cyrano to pick up on the hint. "You've been spying on me! You've been eavesdropping on my conversations with Cyrano."

He made a face. "No, I haven't. We

were in a chat room! I had every right to read what you wrote. I don't understand why you're upset. You liked the things I gave you. You said so. I thought you liked me too."

"I don't even *know* you!"

"Yes, you do. I'm in your French class. We were at the gym riot together—and the basketball game too."

"So was the whole school!"

"But I like you," he said again, moving closer.

Suddenly I was scared. This was exactly what Janice had warned me about. This wasn't my chat room fantasy world. This was real life. This was the school parking lot—very dark and very empty except for me and some lunatic who might attack at any second.

I started backing up. "You just think you like me," I said as calmly as I could.

He shook his head and kept walking toward me.

"No. I really do. We're the same—you and me—kind of on the outside of things.

Loners. Of course, you have your friend, Janice, but I don't really have anybody. Basically, that's what gave me the idea for the chat room. I figured it would be a way to find out what other kids talk about." He shrugged.

"I wanted to know if I was missing anything. Plus I wanted to see if I could actually create a chat room program."

"Well, obviously you did." I faked a smile but continued to back up.

And that's when he lunged. He was much quicker than I expected, and before I could even think about running, he swallowed me in his arms and yanked me right off my feet. My own arms were pinned to my side, so the only thing I could do was scream.

But just as I opened my mouth, Chad spun around, plunked me on the ground again and let me go. I was so shocked my scream came out as a squeak.

"Puddle," he said, nodding to where I'd just been standing. "You were about to step in it."

At first I just stood there with my mouth hanging open. Then I started to laugh, and once I got going, I couldn't stop. It was all so bizarre—Marc turning out to be Cyrano, me coming to the dance because I thought he'd given me the ticket, finding out Chad was my secret admirer, freaking out because I thought he was going to attack me. Then to top everything off, walking into puddles all night.

I sobered up when I realized Chad was staring at me like I had just beamed down from Mars.

I took a few deep breaths before attempting to talk. Then finally I said, "Sorry about that. I wasn't laughing at *you*. Honest. It's just that today's been kind of intense. I'm sorry if I gave you the wrong idea. I didn't mean to lead you on. I thought you were somebody else."

He dropped his head and mumbled, "So you don't like me."

"Yes, I do," I protested, not wanting to

hurt his feelings. "Just not like that. And I bet you don't like me that way either. To tell you the truth, I think we've both been living in a fantasy world. During the day I'm a self-conscious social wannabe and you're a techno-geek—no offense. At night I'm a chat room floozy and you're a cyber-stalker."

His eyes practically popped out of his head. "I wasn't *stalking* you!"

"What would you call it?" I snorted. "You kept your identity hidden, you eavesdropped on my chat room conversations, you followed me around and you sent me secret presents."

He opened his mouth to protest, but then shut it again. After a couple of seconds his face softened into a bashful smile. And suddenly he looked kind of attractive—not hunk-handsome or anything, but really decent.

I realized that I'd never really looked at him before. Maybe there were a lot of things I'd never looked at before.

I smiled back.

"You know," I began hesitantly, "maybe you and I just got off on the wrong foot."

"What do you mean?"

"This whole chat room thing. Think about it. You can't really find out what someone is like by what they say online, can you? You have to get to know them in person. For instance, you think you like me, but what do you really know about me besides that I am magnetically drawn to mud puddles?"

There was that bashful smile again.

Encouraged, I continued. "As for what I know about you—well, let's see. You seem like a nice guy, but all I know for sure is that you're a computer genius and a pretty good poet."

Even in the dark I could see the color flooding Chad's cheeks.

"And you blush when you're embarrassed," I added.

We both snickered.

"So what are you're trying to say?" Chad asked.

I shrugged, suddenly embarrassed. "Do you want to start over?"

It was his turn to shrug. "Sure. Can I walk you to your bus?"

I nodded shyly. "Sure."

chapter twelve

"What on earth happened to you?" my mother said.

I looked down at my soggy wrinkled pants. "A puddle," I replied, shutting the front door.

"Don't you mean lake?"

I shrugged. "It *was* kinda big."

"It must've been. You better get those wet things off before you catch cold." As I started down the hall, she called after me, "And phone Janice. It must be important, because she said to make sure you called no matter how late it was."

As I peeled off my wet clothes, I considered ignoring my mother's message. I was not in the mood to talk to Janice. The day had been crazy, and I needed time to sort it out.

But considering how I'd snapped at her after school when all she was trying to do was help me, the least she deserved was a phone call.

She must have been glued to the thing, because she picked up even before it finished ringing.

"Hi," I said sheepishly.

"Hi." She sounded just as uncomfortable. "I didn't expect you to call so soon." And then cautiously, "Didn't you go to the dance?"

I heaved a huge sigh. "Yes, I went. But I didn't stay." And then I told her the whole story—except the part about Marc being Cyrano. I'd promised I wouldn't mention that to anyone, and though I'd done a lot of dumb things recently, I was still capable of keeping my word.

"As you can see, you were right," I said when there was nothing left to tell. "I should have listened to you. I didn't get raped or murdered or anything, but if Chad had been a different kind of guy, I could have. So go ahead. Say I told you so. I've got it coming."

"I told you so," she said, but her voice was missing the gloating quality I was used to. "I'm also sorry."

I almost dropped the phone. Never in my life had I expected those words to come out of Janice Beasley's mouth.

"Sorry for what?"

"For being such a pill."

"You *were* kinda mean, but considering I wasn't listening, or thinking either for that matter, I can see why you were frustrated."

"The truth is I was jealous," Janice said, catching me completely by surprise. "When you started chatting online, you changed. All of a sudden you had this other life and you were happy."

"But it wasn't real," I reminded her.

It was as if she hadn't heard me. "Then when it looked like you had a boyfriend, I felt totally left out. I wanted what you had. When you said all that stuff this afternoon about me hating the world, it really hurt because it's so not true."

I opened my mouth to argue, but Janice didn't give me the chance.

"I know that's not how it seems, but it's the truth. Don't you see? I know people don't like me. So I act like I don't like them first. That way it doesn't hurt so bad when they reject me."

I was completely stunned. Janice Beasley wanted friends? Impossible. She hated people. There was a long pause as I tried to get my head around what she'd said. It was such a huge confession that I couldn't help thinking about her in a completely different way.

Finally I said, "I'm scared of being rejected too. I'm always afraid I'm going to embarrass myself and people are going to think I'm stupid. So I just kind of hide." Then I started to laugh.

"What's so funny?"

"My technique seems to be working. Nobody knows I exist."

But Janice didn't laugh.

There was another pause, and then I said, "Maybe we need to try something else."

"Oh, yeah," Janice snorted. "Like what?"

"Like just being ourselves. Think about it. We can't do any worse than we're doing right now."

"I guess," Janice mumbled grudgingly.

"We just have to get out there and grab a life."

"Who's?" she muttered.

She hadn't meant it as a joke, but it was funny, and I laughed.

Janice didn't see the humor. "That's fine for you," she sulked, "but everybody hates me."

"That's because you don't give them a chance to like you," I pointed out gently. "When I was chatting online—instead of pulling back like I usually do—I let the real me come out. I didn't worry about making a fool of myself, because I figured nobody would know it was me. The thing is I *didn't* make a fool of myself. The other kids didn't treat me like I was a loser. They seemed to like me just fine. If it could be like that in a chat room, then why not in real life too?"

"But I don't know what to do!" Janice wailed. "How am I supposed to act? What am I supposed to say?"

I sighed. "I'm not sure. But I bet we can figure it out. Maybe we can start going to basketball games and stuff and join some clubs. And we can start talking to other kids instead of hiding from them."

"Or yelling at them?"

Though Janice couldn't see me, I grinned. "That too." Then I did something without even thinking. "Hey, Janice," I said, "there's a new movie playing at Silver City. It started a couple of days ago. I'd really like to see it. What do you say we go together?"

New
Orca Currents Novel

Sewer Rats by Sigmund Brouwer

"The teachers can't do nothing to us," Lisa told him, crossing her arms. *The paintball wars aren't on school property.*

"But—" Micky tried. It was like trying to stop a hurricane.

"Do you think I care what the teachers think?" Lisa asked. "They think we band together because no one else likes us. And we're proud to agree with them, aren't we?"

Micky shrugged. *When people called us losers, it just made our group stronger.*

"It's the Medford gang I care about," Lisa continued. "The Sewer Rats have never lost a paintball war and we're not going to chicken out now."

New
Orca Currents Novel

Laggan Lard Butts by Eric Walters

"That was the bravest thing I ever saw in my whole life," Tanner said.

"Not that brave."

"You're like my hero," Taylor agreed.

"Big deal. It doesn't mean anything. Now we just get to spend more time trying to get people to vote for something that has no chance of winning."

"No chance?" Tanner demanded.

"Yes, no chance."

"I don't believe my ears," Taylor said. "Didn't you listen to the announcements today? A quitter never wins and a Lard Butt never quits. Go, Lard Butts!"

New
Orca Currents Novel

Dog Walker by
Karen Spafford-Fitz

"Just one question, Turk," Mom says. "Why didn't you tell us sooner?"

Mom must have read another parenting article. I can almost see the headline: Getting Your Teen to Open Up to You.

"Well, er...I wanted to get my business running before I said anything. And," I put on my most innocent face, "I had this crazy idea you might think my business was something shady, stupid, or immoral."

I can't tell for sure, but I think Mom and Dad almost look ashamed.

Yes!

Kristin Butcher is scared of chat rooms. For Kristin, writing about things that make her anxious or uncomfortable helps her to confront her fears. Kristin is the best-selling author of a number of books for juveniles and teens, including three Orca Soundings, *The Hemingway Tradition*, *The Trouble with Liberty* and *Zee's Way*. Kristin lives in Victoria, British Columbia.